(This book is for children, ages 3-7 years.)

Included in this book are sensory activities and creative questions for children. Educators and parents have the opportunity to use this book as they see fit. And kids can color and draw anywhere *they* see fit!

**Outstanding Features**

*This story is easy enough for the youngest readers to read themselves (or for educators and parents to read to them). Its simple, universal messages inherently teach respect for nature and its many unique creatures. It may also be used in these ways:*

*As a method for involving young learners in early science related to nature and marine environments.

*As an outstanding (and fun!) tool to give prior to a marine field trip.

*As a year's-end activity book to keep students stimulated during vacation months and even before.

# Angel's Shore

"Hello! My name is Angel. I live in Heaven. Heaven can be the sky *or* a beautiful place that makes you happy."

Draw *your* heaven.

"Our yard is buried in sand and beach grass."

(I love drawing my heaven.)

How do your feet feel when walking on summer sand? How do they feel on winter sand? Write your answers, *or* draw a picture of walking on summer or winter sand.

"When it's sunny, the grass shines."

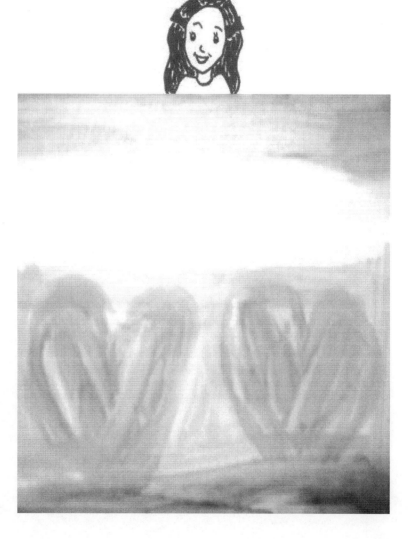

How would you draw sunshine on grass? Try drawing your own shiny grass.

"When it rains, the grass dances."

(The squiggly lines are my dancing grass.)

What do you hear when it rains on grass?

"A short stretch away, is an ocean."

(The path to it is on the lower-right.)

What treasures are in the ocean? Draw what you imagine. Strange shells, a mermaid's box of stones and pearls, magical dolphins playing tag -- anything!

"The ocean has many animal friends."

What do fish and crabs think? Pretend you are a fish or crab swimming or crawling in the ocean.

"But my favorite friend is a girl named Ashley."

Do you have a special friend? It can be a human or animal. Draw a picture of your friend.

"Ashley and I run and laugh through summer sand …"

Play a game of Tag: The first person (or animal) who is "it" must chase his/her friend. Use a hand to touch-tag your friend. Once you do, your friend becomes "it" and must tag *you*. If your friend is an animal, expect a body-bump!

16

"… saying hello to our wild friends.
Crabs run through tide pools, their long eyes peering up."

Who are your wild friends? They might be fish, far-away seals or whales,
snails, birds, crickets, butterflies -- any outdoor creatures.

What would it be like to be a crab in water peering up at a person? Draw a picture!

"Snails rest on big, parent rocks. Snails can't hear, so they rely on other senses. They must love feeling sun warm their shells while snug inside."

Create your own kind of shell home: Hang a sheet or blanket over a small table. Put it in a sunny spot and crawl in!

"When we touch the snails, they're glued to their sturdy, smooth home."

Snails have a flap inside their shell's opening that they can open and close!

"Oysters are the tide-pool sloths."

Did you know a *sloth* is a slow, hairy mammal that climbs trees?

"Sometimes, Ashley and I wade deep into the sea."

Imagine what animals you might find deep in the ocean.

"Our fish friends can be seen in the ocean."

Did you know that in diffcrent kinds of light, the ocean seems to change color?

Draw and color what an ocean looks like during a cloudy day, then during a sunny day.

"And *my* favorites are the distant seals,

Write down what you would do if you found a big rock while swimming. Sit on it and listen to sounds around you? Look through the water to find crabs, fish, and snails? Or enjoy distant sights of ocean, sand, and trees?

"There, the seals sun themselves. Imagine being on that island rock … "

… with just quiet.

"At day's end, Ashley and I sit (and sometimes lay) down
in soft sand next to each other."

Do this with a friend. In the warm sun, it feels calming. When you and your
friend are quiet, what do you hear? Tell each other to see if one heard
something the other missed.

"Then we wave our arms and legs back and forth,
making sand angels."

Try this with your friend.

"We've made our marks."

"After we've left, the tide rolls in."

"It claims our sandy marks,
and takes away a part of us."

Share with your friend how this makes you feel. Find some rocks and shells
and place them far away from the tide where they will last long.

"But the next morning, nature has her own way of giving it all back. Shore beauty looks just as it did before."

"As I said, I live in Heaven."

**Sara Webb Quest** writes, and draws on Cape Cod in a cottage by the sea. She lives with a husband, daughter, and cat. She is the author of the *"Aydil Vice"* children's books and her stories have been published in *Fandangle*, *Society of Children's Book Writers & Illustrators Bulletin*, *Cape Cod Parent & Child*, *Prime Time Cape Cod*, and *Woman's World*.

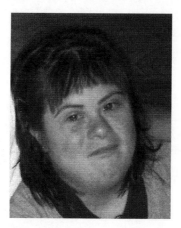

**Cynthia Goldberg** lives on Cape Cod and works as an assistant preschool teacher at Stepping Stones Too in Mashpee. As a multi-talented young lady, she has been featured several times in the *Cape Cod Times* for her contributions to life on Cape Cod. As an art student at the Cotuit Center for the Arts, one of her images was selected by the Cape Cod Chapter of the American Heart Association to be their design for the 2008 season. Several years before in 2002, one of her lines of poetry was chosen by the Cape Cod Women's Club to be the saying on their tee-shirt. Currently, she gets continual recognition as a Global Speaker for the Special Olympics in Massachusetts

35

Made in the USA
Lexington, KY
15 November 2012